JEREMY'S CHRISTMAS Journey

SCOTT A. JOHNSON

MUSIC COMPOSED BY
Lyle Hadlock, Julie Hawkins, & Jonah Hadlock

SWEETWATER
BOOKS

AN IMPRINT OF CEDAR FORT, INC.
SPRINGVILLE, UTAH

© 2012 Scott A. Johnson
Music © 2012 Lyle Hadlock, Julie Hawkins, and Jonah Hadlock

All rights reserved.

No part of this book may be reproduced in any form whatsoever, whether by graphic, visual, electronic, film, microfilm, tape recording, or any other means, without prior written permission of the publisher, except in the case of brief passages embodied in critical reviews and articles.

This is a work of fiction. The characters, names, incidents, places, and dialogue are products of the author's imagination, and are not to be construed as real. The opinions and views expressed herein belong solely to the author and do not necessarily represent the opinions or views of Cedar Fort, Inc. Permission for the use of sources, graphics, and photos is also solely the responsibility of the author.

ISBN 13: 978-1-4621-1122-0 (Book)
ISBN 13: 978-1-4621-1124-4 (Book & CD Set)

Published by Sweetwater Books, an imprint of Cedar Fort, Inc., 2373 W. 700 S., Springville, UT 84663
Distributed by Cedar Fort, Inc., www.cedarfort.com

LIBRARY OF CONGRESS CATALOGING-IN-PUBLICATION DATA

Johnson, Scott A., 1976- author.
 Jeremy's Christmas journey / Scott A. Johnson.
    pages cm
 Summary: For Jeremy, Christmas is just another reminder that he'll never be able to enjoy the things that come so easily to other children. Then one night he has a dream that will change everything.
 ISBN 978-1-4621-1122-0
 1. Children with disabilities--Fiction. 2. Dreams--Fiction. 3. Jesus Christ--Apparitions and miracles--Fiction. 4. Christmas stories.
 I. Title.

 PS3610.O3768J47 2012
 813'.6--dc23

                    2012027106

Cover design by Erica Dixon
Cover design © 2012 by Lyle Mortimer
Edited and typeset by Kelley Konzak

Printed in the United States of America

10 9 8 7 6 5 4 3 2 1

TO MY FAMILY, ESPECIALLY MY WIFE, WHO MADE CONSIDERABLE SACRIFICES for me to complete this project. To the heavenly help of inspiration and courage I received to finish this journey. And to the great support and assistance of my parents, Lyle Hadlock, Jonah Hadlock, Julie Hawkins, McKay Crockett, Susan Alleman, and Marta and Adam Smith. Thanks to all of my many friends, supporters, and family who helped make my vision a reality!

PRAISE FOR JEREMY'S CHRISTMAS JOURNEY

"Jeremy's Christmas Journey is a delightful story to add a new level of worship to your Christmas celebrations. This book would be a wonderful gift to present to your seeking friends and family!"

— Meagan Myhren-Bennett, *Blooming with Books*

"A faithless and bitter crippled boy receives a Christmas miracle only his Savior could bestow. New music from Lyle Hadlock, Julie Hawkins, and Jonah Hadlock make this book a treasure."

— Kjirstin Youngberg, actress

The Journey

IT WAS A BEAUTIFUL CHRISTMAS EVE DAY. THE GROUND was covered with a fresh blanket of fluffy, white snow, which had fallen overnight, continuing into the early-morning hours. The air was crisp, the sun was shining, and the cloudless sky was brilliant blue.

Children were playing snow games as they laughed and enjoyed the newness of the day. They were building snowmen with sticks for arms, a carrot for a nose, and rocks for eyes, mouth, and shirt buttons. Laughter and shrieks of excitement echoed from the rooftops as children sledded down makeshift hills created with great effort. Ice-covered snow shovels and empty wheelbarrows were now set aside. Snow angels disrupted the otherwise velvety-smooth snow.

Great excitement appeared on the children's faces while they hurled tightly packed snowballs as part of a spirited snowball fight. The little ones were content just to watch the goings-on, in awe of the beautiful surroundings.

The children were parading around with large smiles, and all seemed to be having such a wonderful time. All, that is, except Jeremy Hatfield. Jeremy sat in his bedroom scowling as he gazed out the window at the children. To him, being stuck inside, staring through the window, was like looking through the bars of a prison—a prison he so desperately desired to escape. He watched them glumly, wishing he too could be outside instead of confined to the wheelchair he had been in most of his life. He almost couldn't bear watching the other children enjoying themselves while he was stuck inside. It just didn't seem fair.

Jeremy became disabled at such a young age he almost couldn't remember what it was like to run and play with other children, let alone walk or enjoy a stroll through fresh snow. He tried hard to remember the feeling of standing on his own two feet, the feeling of wind rushing through his hair as he ran, the exhilaration of dancing, and the temporary flight of jumping. All those things seemed a distant memory, something he would never experience again. It made him angry to think of all the children who took these simple, everyday events for granted. For a moment he wished his condition on one of them. He sought to trade places and be free of his affliction. He shook his head in disgust, knowing that what he was wishing wasn't right.

As a toddler, Jeremy had been the victim of a debilitating car accident. While he and his mother were driving home from the grocery store, a drunk driver failed to stop at a red light, plowing into the side of the family minivan. Unfortunately for Jeremy, it was the side he was sitting on. He couldn't remember much about the accident nor the frantic care he received at the crash site, but his mom said the firemen had struggled for an hour to free Jeremy's legs from the twisted metal and broken glass. In fact, the emergency personnel that responded had said it was a miracle he was alive. *Some miracle,* Jeremy often thought. Sometimes he pitied himself to the point that he wished he had not survived the accident.

This thought put him at odds with his parents, who perceived him as a miracle. Instead Jeremy chose to think of his situation as a tragedy. His mom considered Jeremy not only a miracle but also a gift from God, especially since she was unable to conceive any more children. In some ways, this made Jeremy even more upset about his circumstances. He felt that he was a disappointment to his parents, a misfortune or burden to them. *They deserve a child without any limitations, a child who doesn't place such a great weight on them,* he thought.

His mom and dad had spent endless hours sitting next to his hospital bed, hoping and praying for Jeremy to recover as he floated in and out of consciousness, clinging desperately to life. His mom held his hand for hours, lovingly stroking his head and manipulating the joints in his arms and legs to avoid the muscle atrophy and stiffening of joints so common among coma patients. His father read him stories and sang him his favorite songs. Both had placed their lives on hold with great sacrifice, turning their complete focus on Jeremy and his recovery. Together, they had knelt by his bed many times in fervent prayer, petitioning God to spare their son. His mom always told him they could have filled a river with the tears they shed, hoping and waiting for Jeremy to heal.

The nurses and doctors provided thoughtful and kind care, slowly nursing Jeremy back to health as his loved ones waited in eager anticipation for him to regain full consciousness. Those who cared for him grew attached to this precious toddler and began to treat him as one of their own children. Often, one of them would come in on his or her day off to bring him balloons or check on his condition. Some even relieved Jeremy's mother and spent time holding his hand while gazing upon him lovingly. It was not uncommon to find tear-filled eyes when his mother returned from her short respite.

When Jeremy finally awoke from the coma, he had a long road to recovery. In all, Jeremy spent six weeks in the intensive care unit, underwent several surgeries to repair his badly crushed legs, and endured many grueling physical therapy sessions. But, despite all of these efforts and the best that modern medicine had to offer, he was never able to walk again. The accident left him paralyzed from the waist down. Curiously, no medical reason had been discovered for his paralysis, but the doctors assumed that there was some spinal cord damage that could not be detected in the MRI and CT scans. The only other possibility they considered was that a neurological anomaly had occurred during the traumatic event that left him unable to use his legs.

This fact gave his mother and father hope that the condition was still reversible and that one day Jeremy would regain the use of the lower half of his body. Jeremy held on to this same desire at the beginning, but after months with no apparent progress, he gave up, choosing to accept that his body was damaged beyond repair.

JEREMY'S *Christmas* JOURNEY

His parents tirelessly researched paralysis and sought opinions from many experts but had been unsuccessful in helping Jeremy overcome his burden.

From then on, his mother and father always insisted they were just grateful he was alive. Many times they had endured the agonizing dread that he would never regain full consciousness—thoughts no parents should have to confront. As they looked at the pictures from the accident and the severity of the damage to the family minivan, it confirmed in their minds that it was a miracle he even survived. His mother always declared that Jeremy had angels watching over and protecting him, giving him comfort in his time of need. She emphatically believed that he wouldn't have made it had he not had heavenly support. She felt in her heart that Jeremy had been preserved for a special purpose.

Jeremy tried hard to adjust to his new condition, but it was hard for someone as young as he was to rely on others in all aspects of his life. When he started school, he had to have classmates push him in his wheelchair to the lunchroom or assemblies and, even more embarrassing, to the bathroom. Most children accepted him, even befriended him, trying to include him in their regular activities as much as possible, but other children made fun of him and called him names that hurt Jeremy deeply. Many times he feigned sick just to avoid the embarrassment and humiliation he felt at school.

He didn't understand why he had this hardship placed upon him, a hardship that precluded him from being able to do things the other children could, and it frustrated him greatly. He felt inadequate and inferior to the other children as he received help to carry out tasks others his age easily accomplished. To him, the others had so much freedom compared to him, freedom he felt they took for granted.

At school he didn't know what to do with himself during recess, when the other children were playing outside. So he usually asked to stay inside with the teacher and help her in any way he could. He cleaned the blackboard as high up as he could reach, helped pass out papers for the next assignment, and did anything else to keep his mind off the fun the other children were having. Often his jealousy would cause him to lash out at his schoolmates, further compounding his difficulties and ostracizing him from the friendships he so desperately desired and needed.

Jeremy was an excellent student, rarely receiving less than perfect scores in school. He had little ability to play like the other children, so he spent a lot of time reading and studying. His intelligence level was at least equal to those a grade higher than him, and he was always at the top of his class in academics. Some of the students called him "teacher's pet," which intensified his resentment for able-bodied children.

He felt sorry for himself as he looked out the window at all the children who were enjoying themselves in the snow. *They don't even care about me or know what it's like to be in this condition*, he thought to himself with a sour expression growing on his face. *If only they could get a taste of what I go through, then they would show more concern for me.*

Christmas day didn't bring him the same joy it brought most children. It reminded him of all the gifts the other children would receive

JEREMY'S *Christmas* JOURNEY

that he would never enjoy: the bikes and skateboards, the jump ropes and footballs—his mind conjured a plethora of items that he couldn't make use of. *I could have been a great football player or a world-class sprinter if only that drunk would have taken a cab that night.* He continued his thoughts as fierce anger built up for the man that had driven drunk that day.

Jeremy often had trouble sleeping at night, which led him to thoughts about what he would say to this selfish person if he ever met him and got the chance. Forgiveness was out of the question. He would let him have a piece of his mind! Tell him how he had destroyed his life and crushed his dreams. *If only my legs worked, I would give him a giant kick to the shin,* he thought. Jeremy turned his wheelchair around suddenly, no longer desiring to look out the window, and placed his head in his hands. His emotions took control, and his eyes welled up with tears.

He recalled the conversation he frequently had with his father: "Some things we don't understand, but they are meant for our own good and growth. Look at Job," his dad would say. "He had many trials and not once cursed God. Instead he chose to learn from his trials and stayed faithful. God gives us trials not because he doesn't care for us or love us, but because they are opportunities to learn and become stronger. He answers all prayers, Jeremy. Sometimes they just may not be answered in the way or the time we want. We need to trust in the Lord's plan for us. He knows best."

Jeremy wondered what good could result from being confined to a wheelchair. *I can't do much good at all,* he thought. "Surely nothing good could come of a boy being confined to a wheelchair," he muttered out loud.

Just then the doorbell rang. He gathered himself quickly and wiped away the tears from his moist eyes, not wanting anyone to see that he had been crying. Despite this action, his puffy, red eyes betrayed the truth. He waited a few moments to calm and collect himself, then wheeled his way out his bedroom door and down the hall. His mother was just opening the door as he reached the end of the hall, and there on the porch stood his grandparents. Their smiling faces and kind demeanor always lifted his spirits, and he was glad to see them. He almost let a smile replace his frown but prevented a full smile from developing, instead ending with a half-hearted grin. He wheeled closer to them as they entered the living room, fighting back the urge to bury his head in their shoulders and cry.

"How's my little champ?" his grandpa asked, wrapping his warm, firm arms around him with a tight embrace. His grandfather always made him feel special. Jeremy felt as if he were Grandpa's favorite, but then again, so did all of his cousins. His grandfather treated all his grandchildren as though they were his favorite and had a way about him of making each one feel better and uplifted. He had a way of building self-esteem that was unequaled.

Not far behind Grandpa, Grandma was carrying something in her hands—a present wrapped in shiny red wrapping paper with golden ribbon and a glistening green bow. She seemed to know the right words to make him feel better no matter the circumstances. She was so kind and radiated an unconditional love. She reached out her free

JEREMY'S *Christmas* JOURNEY

hand and tussled his light brown hair with her fingers. This touch gave rise to the feelings she experienced as she sat next to Jeremy's hospital bed, gazing into his unresponsive face, hoping for a miracle. In the hospital, she had longed for him to open his beautiful blue eyes and show his dazzling smile, dimples and all.

Jeremy's demeanor lightened a little as he wondered what might lie hidden beneath all the shiny wrapping paper. He hoped it would be more than the book he got last year. While he appreciated the reading material that gave him a brief escape from his wheelchair-confined world, it just wasn't what he wanted.

"Here you go, Grandson," Grandma began. "You might as well open it now. We aren't going to be here tomorrow." Grandma looked at Jeremy's mother as if asking permission. Jeremy's mother smiled and nodded her approval as she turned and headed into the kitchen.

Jeremy's grandma had spent many hours with him in the hospital, caressing his head while speaking encouraging words and helping his mother flex his joints to keep them from stiffening. This experience created an enduring bond between them. She always made him feel important and special by the way she treated him and the consistent love and care that she showed him. He didn't remember much about his experiences in the hospital, but he vaguely remembered her heartfelt prayers as she stroked his head, kneeling next to his hospital bed.

"Thanks, Grandma and Grandpa," Jeremy said as he began to remove the green bow and ribbon from the present with great anticipation. His eyes were wide and focused on the prize before him as his grandparents joyfully looked on. When the wrapping paper was finally removed, it revealed a new football game for his PlayStation 3. His eyes quickly turned from anticipation to defeated sadness, his whole body caving in with despair. It wasn't that he didn't want this game—in fact, it was one of his favorites—but it brought to remembrance the reality that he could not play real football. He said thank you and tried to muster a smile and maintain his previous excitement, but it ended up looking like a grimace, the forced smile often seen on picture day at school.

He longed to be on the football field with the other boys instead of just playing football on a video game console. He absolutely knew he would be great at it, if he had the ability to run. He was as tall or taller than most of the other boys in his class, and his upper body displayed the muscles he developed from moving himself from place to place in a wheelchair. Jeremy was a huge sports fan, following both college and professional football. As he watched it on television, he often dreamed of being on the field and catching the game-winning touchdown. But those were only dreams, dreams that he had come to accept would never happen.

"It's time for dinner," his mother said, breaking the silence that had descended over the room. She turned and headed to the dining room, where she was undoubtedly applying the finishing touches to the meal. She was a wonderful cook and an attentive hostess. For the first time, Jeremy became aware of the delicious aroma that filled the house.

Jeremy had started to wheel himself toward the dining room table

JEREMY'S *Christmas* JOURNEY

when the front door opened. It was his dad, dressed in warm winter clothes. He removed his gloves, hat, boots, and heavy coat. He had been shoveling the walks. His cheeks and nose were rosy red, reminding Jeremy of Santa Claus.

His dad smiled and moved toward Jeremy, grabbing hold of the back of the wheelchair and pushing him to the end of the table. He patted Jeremy on the shoulder and gave him a nod, then took his own seat. For a moment he kept his gaze on Jeremy as if translating his demeanor, then gave him a look as if he knew Jeremy was suffering. Jeremy looked at his dad and gave a brief smile of thanks, then turned his attention to the table.

The table was covered with the traditional Christmas Eve meal—a succulent roasted turkey, warm mashed potatoes and gravy, candied yams, green beans, homemade orange rolls, and Jeremy's favorite of all: pumpkin pie with whipped cream. Jeremy's mouth began to water as he gazed at the delicious feast. His stomach gave a slight growl, and for the first time he realized he felt hungry.

Jeremy's father looked at everyone, ensuring he had their attention, then bowed his head and folded his arms. Following the blessing on the food, they all began to feast on the meal that had been so lovingly prepared. Jeremy's mother gave him a wink as she placed an extra-large portion of pumpkin pie on his desert plate. His eyes widened in eagerness to eat it. He ate the main course quickly, not wanting to wait another moment to eat pie.

Despite the magnificent feast, Jeremy remained quiet and sullen, lamenting over his lack of opportunity to be outside with the other children. He couldn't shake the pessimistic emotions he was feeling. He felt as though a black cloud was hovering over him. His grandparents and parents carried on conversations about the weather, politics, and so forth, hardly even noticing Jeremy's gloomy temperament. The only thing that slightly cheered his spirits was the taste of his creamy and delicious piece of pumpkin pie. His mouth salivated as he lifted his first forkful to his mouth. He ate the pie slowly, savoring every bite. When he finished, he asked to be excused from the table. He didn't want to be around others; instead he wanted to be alone, where he could sulk in solitude without having to control his emotions. He slowly wheeled himself into the family room, making sure that he didn't face the windows so he wouldn't have to look at the other children enjoying themselves again.

Despite his best efforts, he soon dropped back into despondency. Even though he wasn't looking at the other children, he knew they were out there, and he occasionally heard an exuberant shout as they played. He couldn't take these feelings anymore. He peeked out the window, his mind daydreaming, pretending he was playing with the other children. He imagined he was sledding or building a snowman, anything but stuck in the house on Christmas Eve—and worse, in a wheelchair. He almost loathed the other children, again wishing his circumstances on one of them. He yearned to have their abilities, if for only one day.

His dad came in the room without Jeremy noticing and lovingly placed his arms around him from behind. His dad seemed to have a sixth sense and close connection to Jeremy's feelings. He could always

JEREMY'S *Christmas* JOURNEY

tell when Jeremy was down and needed his spirits lifted.

"Some things we don't understand, son . . ." his dad began.

"But they are meant for our own good," Jeremy finished his father's sentence. "I know, Dad. I just wish that for even one day I could play out there with the other kids. It's just not fair!" Jeremy's emotions were becoming more apparent, and he wondered if he would be able to control them much longer. A lump was forming in his throat, and he could feel his lip quivering.

"Someday you'll be able to walk, son, I just know it. Have some faith in Christ."

Jeremy didn't say anything, but inside he thought to himself, *Yeah right*. He rolled his eyes in disgust, attempting to hide his face.

"It's time for the Christmas story from Luke," his father said as his mother and grandparents gathered in the family room. His grandparents sat on the couch holding hands lovingly, eagerness shining from their eyes. The love they shared was obvious. His mother sat next to his father with her head on his shoulder so she could read with him. His dad opened his well-worn scriptures and began to read. "And it came to pass in those days, that there went out a decree from Caesar Augustus, that all the world should be taxed . . ."

Jeremy's mind began to wander as his father continued. He thought of the events involved in the Christmas story. Angelic visitations, Mary's miraculous conception, Joseph's understanding. He pondered the animals that were in the manger. Did they truly know the baby they were beholding was more than just a baby? Had shepherds really seen an angel and followed a wondrous star to behold him? He questioned whether such an amazing tale could even be true. It was hard for him to comprehend how the Son of God could be born into this world, in such humble circumstances as a manger, and then go on to become such a great man. *The Son of God shouldn't be born in a manger, he should be born in a palace*, he thought. He wondered, if such a being really existed, why he would let him be wheelchair-bound. Why would Christ allow people to suffer if he had the power to heal them? Surely a just person wouldn't allow that! As his father continued the story, he began to doubt the reality of the events. He thought, *There is no way that any of this happened. It just can't be true. This is just a story that someone made up to make people feel good.* He shook his head in disbelief, temporarily caught up in his thoughts and not paying attention to the words his father was reading.

He looked up just as his father finished reading the story, hoping no one had seen his contemplative disposition. As he scanned the room, he saw tears in his mother's eyes and watched them trail down her cheeks. She always cried when his father read the Christmas story. Jeremy was partly ashamed to look at his mother, knowing the faith and belief in Jesus Christ she held so dear. He turned his wheelchair toward the hall in shame, no longer able to look at the people he loved so dearly as they recollected the story of the man he clearly doubted existed.

"Where are you going?" his mother asked.

"I'm sorry, Mom. I just don't feel very good. I think I'll just go to bed. Good night, Mom and Dad. Good night, Grandma and Grandpa."

His parents and grandparents exchanged concerned looks, but

JEREMY'S *Christmas* JOURNEY

they remained motionless, as if frozen in time, not knowing how they could comfort or help Jeremy. They all looked as though they expected one of the others to do or say something. Finally they did the only thing they could think of and wished him good night.

"Good night and merry Christmas!" they said in unison as he slowly wheeled down the hall.

When Jeremy got to his room, he opened the middle drawer of his dresser, taking out his favorite San Francisco 49ers pajamas his mother had recently sewn him. He started the tedious undertaking of undressing, struggling especially to get his bottoms on. This took great effort to accomplish, but he wanted to become more independent, so he insisted on doing it himself. It allowed him to feel more self-sufficient. When he was finally finished dressing, he let out a sigh of relief.

Slowly he wheeled over to the side of his bed and set the brakes on his wheelchair. His head was hanging in despair as he pulled with all his might to sit on the edge of the bed. Once there, he grabbed his lower legs and swung them onto the bed. He pulled the covers from the bottom of his bed up tight to his chest, preparing for the cold night ahead. He shivered slightly from the chill of his cold covers and pillow and then settled in, tired and frustrated.

However, sleep did not come easily or quickly. He couldn't seem to get the thoughts of the Christmas story out of his head. His thoughts were so fixed on the validity of the Christmas story, he didn't even think about Santa Claus coming tonight. He lay in bed, staring at the ceiling, for what seemed to him hours, debating all of the facts of the

Christmas story, mulling over all the minute details again and again. Soon his eyes felt heavy. No longer able to fight the ensuing exhaustion, he gradually drifted to sleep.

Unexpectedly, he found himself in an unfamiliar place. He surveyed his surroundings with great anxiety. He could see he was in a spacious, ancient building surrounded by people who seemed to be engrossed in the proceedings going on before them. The bare and plain walls appeared to be made of stone or clay. The floor was dirt. The ceiling was very primitive, covered in sticks and straw. Jeremy wanted to scream, but as he opened his mouth, no sound escaped.

He was seated on a long bench, among several other benches, each occupied with hosts of people. At the front of the room was a solitary stool on a slightly raised platform. To the side of the platform, a formidable-looking man sat on another stool situated behind a small table. The man craned his head to see around the gathering crowd as if anticipating someone's arrival.

Soldiers dressed in ancient military apparel stood resolutely to either side of the formidable man. At the front of the room and on Jeremy's left, two more men were staring straight ahead as if unaware of their surroundings. To his right, eight more men were huddled together, conversing emphatically. They looked as if they were debating or discussing something of great importance. Just then one of the eight men moved to the front of the room and began to speak. He looked directly at the man behind the table.

"Your Honor, the prosecution rests. Our case against this Jesus, the pretended prophet, is established suitably and without a doubt. He

JEREMY'S *Christmas* JOURNEY

is not the Son of God, as his so-called disciples profess, but merely an impostor who, through the cunning of the devil, has deceived many. He is a blasphemer, a liar, a disturber of the peace, and a fraud. We now turn the time over to the defense, where they, like Jesus, will try to use trickery and illusion to establish their futile and pretended counterargument. We appeal to you, Your Honor and members of the courtroom, to avoid letting the foolery of the defense sway you to believe in Jesus, for anyone who believes their words will bring the condemnation of God upon himself." The man pointed a finger across the crowd as if to intimidate, then sat down, receiving pats on the back and looks of congratulation from the seven men next to him.

Where am I? Jeremy thought to himself. He glanced at his surroundings once more, quite sure he had never been in this place before. Concern was apparent on his face, like that of a child lost in a crowd. Yet he felt that he needed to be here, almost as if he had been invited to attend the event. He rubbed his eyes to make sure they were not deceiving him and then determined he must be dreaming, dreaming of an event taking place long before his birth.

Jeremy watched as one of the men to the left appeared to come out of deep thought, then arise and begin to speak. "Your Honor, and ladies and gentlemen of the courtroom, the prosecution is misguided in their condemnation of Jesus, for he is the Christ, the very Son of God. We have the scriptures and the prophets of old that testify of him. We have the many miracles that he performed. But most of all, we have the people whose lives he touched during his mortal ministry as witnesses that he is the Son of God, even Jehovah, the Messiah, and the Savior of the world. We have many who are willing to come and testify of this fact, despite the threats and intimidation they have endured." He paused shortly, glaring at the prosecution as if to accuse them. "As our first witness to testify before the court, we call Mary the mother of Jesus."

Great gasps were heard from the onlookers in the room, and some jeered and hissed. Jeremy turned as the door to the courtroom opened and a middle-aged woman was escorted to the front and placed on the stool seated on the platform. He looked upon her intently, admiring her striking beauty. Though she was obviously aged, she projected a glow around her that made her beautiful. Her eyes revealed a great tenderness and love—a motherly love—yet also unhidden, her eyes hinted at the heavy burden she seemed to carry. It was apparent she was grieving a great loss. Tears seemed to be welling up at the corners of her eyes. She was obviously uncomfortable, almost frightened.

"Are you the mother of Jesus, who was born in Bethlehem and recently crucified at Golgotha?" the man began.

"Yes, sir," was her simple but firm answer as she looked him straight in the eyes.

"Was Joseph, who was your espoused husband, his father?"

"Joseph was my husband, and he appeared as Jesus's father to many while he was upon the earth," she started, "but the truth must be told that Jesus's father was God." Her conviction that her statement was true was visible in her face.

A loud roar of boos and yells immediately rose throughout the courtroom. Angry faces glowered at Mary, while some shook their

JEREMY'S *Christmas* JOURNEY

fists or pointed angrily. Jeremy thought for a moment that the crowd was enraged enough to mob her and carry her out of the courtroom. He shuddered as he thought of the stoning he had learned about in Sunday School, hoping that he would not have to witness one personally. Mary looked over the crowd, unwavering and with an air of confidence. Jeremy was surprised that she didn't cower and press against the wall behind her.

"This is blasphemy. Remove her from the court!" came an angry voice from the crowd.

Another shouted, "Stone her!" as he shook an angry finger in her direction.

Mary looked sternly at her accusers. The look on her face made it clear that this was not the first time she had experienced this treatment. It was evident that she was used to this type of behavior from others. Then, suddenly, she appeared as if she had received great strength, as though someone had entered the room to fortify and sustain her. Unable to hold back her testimony any longer, she rose to her feet and began to speak.

More Than My Son
(The Testimony of Mary the Mother of Jesus)

As the angel delivered his message,
I was shocked and in great awe
That I was chosen to carry
The precious Son of God.

I knew that this baby was special
As I held him to my breast
A glow shone brightly about him
I surely can attest.

Chorus:
I knew he came for a purpose
I did not quite understand.
His mission would take his life.
It was all part of the plan.

This is my testimony.
The mother of the Son of God.
And so in like manner,
We must come to know him too.

With broken heart and contrite spirit,
Walking in the path he trod,
And gain a testimony of his mission.
The Son of God.

JEREMY'S *Christmas* JOURNEY

As I pondered his wonderful message,
Wond'ring what my Son would be.
He was more than my baby;
The Son of God was he.

On the day that his body was broken
I wept beneath his feet.
He returned to his Father in Heaven,
To take his rightful seat.

Chorus

The crowd was quiet and hushed, a significant change from only moments before. Looks of astonishment and amazement were visible among the crowd gathered to witness the event. No one dared to speak or contend with the power of Mary's testimony. Even the prosecution seemed bewildered, unsure of what to say or do next.

Jeremy was perplexed also. Mary's strong testimony had touched him, filling him with great warmth in his bosom. An overwhelming sensation of love was growing inside him, a love that seemed tangible. It was a feeling he had not experienced in a great while, but it reminded him of the love his mother and father had for him. He felt peaceful and calm as he processed the powerful influence Mary's testimony had had on him. He almost wished he could believe her testimony, but he wasn't ready to accept it quite yet. Doubt and anger were deeply entrenched in his mind, and he couldn't let go of those feelings yet. He was not about to let one compelling testimony overcome years of bitterness.

He continued to stare at her beautiful eyes, drawn to them almost uncontrollably. Finally Mary raised her eyes enough to notice his gaze. He quickly turned away and looked down, hanging his head in shame. Jeremy was frightened. He felt as though her powerful vision had the potential to penetrate his mind and read his thoughts. He couldn't bear to meet her gaze again, knowing the doubt that was deeply entrenched in his mind. He couldn't tolerate the burden of Mary knowing that he doubted her son's validity as Savior of the world. He felt awkward, wanting to be alone. He wished he could flee the situation, flee to a place where he could become invisible,

JEREMY'S *Christmas* JOURNEY

completely hidden from her seemingly all-seeing gaze.

Jeremy shut his eyes tightly, screwing his face up and hoping that he would appear back in his room, where he could escape this unpleasant situation. When he finally gathered enough courage to open one eye slightly, he checked to see if the coast was clear. To his great disappointment, he was still in the courtroom.

One of the defense lawyers started speaking, "We have no further questions for Mary, Your Honor. Her testimony is a powerful witness of her Son, as will be the testimony of the others who will speak here this day. Mary is a good woman, an honest woman; no one can deny this fact. There is no reason to doubt the validity of her testimony."

One of the eight prosecuting lawyers hissed and then acted as if he would say something. He looked at the crowd, then back at Mary, anger evident in his expression. At last he turned to the judge and spoke, "The prosecution has no questions for Mary at this time. We offer our condolences that she has lost her son but urge the court to remember that her words are that of a mother, a mother who would do anything to protect her son, despite the fact that he no longer exists. She has much to gain by testifying that her son was more than a common man. We request that you remember this and discount her testimony altogether." The man unconsciously fidgeted with the shawl around his shoulders. He was obviously frustrated and perturbed.

Jeremy hung his head in shame, not wanting to make eye contact with Mary again. Though he did not personally know her, he felt as if he should protect her honor and come to her aid. She seemed like such an honest and kind woman; certainly she didn't deserve such harsh treatment. He wished he could gather the courage to help her. *But what could a boy in a wheelchair do anyway?*, he thought.

After what seemed like several minutes but was likely only a few moments, his curiosity got the best of him and he had to look at her again. He slowly raised his head and peered at the platform. It was empty. Mary was gone, and though he was somewhat relieved by this fact, he also felt deep sorrow. He looked frantically around the room to find her, but it was too late. She had been escorted from the room and was nowhere to be found. How he wished he could have talked to her further and asked her so many questions, questions that might have answered the doubt that lay deeply ingrained in his mind. He wondered if she would be able to give him the comfort he urgently desired. Alas, he had lost the opportunity to find out the answer to these unspoken queries, and a deep feeling of regret filled his body.

Just then he saw one of the defense lawyers stand up again and motion to the door. "The defense calls James, the brother of Jesus, as our next witness."

The doors opened again, and a man came forward dressed in well-worn, simple clothes and sandals. It appeared as though he had been on a long journey with little rest. His hands and face were weathered from the sun, and his body displayed signs of a lifetime of hard physical labor. He was muscular and toned. From Jeremy's vantage point, James appeared much taller than most of the other men in the room. His countenance gave a warm glow that invited all who gazed upon him to smile as he walked humbly forward, not looking in either

JEREMY'S *Christmas* JOURNEY

direction, simply focusing on the task ahead of him. Once seated on the stool, he sat resolutely. His posture was tall and straight as he looked straight forward toward the back wall as if he were looking past the people in the audience. His demeanor appeared almost kingly, as if he were sitting upon a throne and ruling over his subjects.

The defense began to question him. "State your name for the records of this court please."

"I am James, son of Joseph and Mary, and the half-brother of Jesus," he said.

The defense continued, "Was anything different about your brother growing up?"

"Jesus was as most other children, though we all knew he was more than just a normal boy. He had a way about him that drew you in and made you want to be near him. He made friends easily when we were young because of this. In fact, I am ashamed to admit that the attention he recieved often made me jealous. He also acted differently. He was inherently good, always well-mannered, constantly serving others, and thinking of others' needs before his own. I could discern that he knew he was here for a purpose, a purpose he never deviated from. Everything he did prepared him for what he became—"

"This isn't storytelling time! We care not for your memories or your gossip. How is this relevant to this trial?" one of the prosecuting lawyers yelled out, interrupting James.

James looked at the man sternly. Their eyes met and locked, as if in a staring contest. Neither was willing to move his eyes away for

25

fear of losing. Finally, the lawyer relented, looking toward his companions as if pleading for help and support.

"And do you believe that this brother of yours was the Christ, the One prophesied of who would save his people?" the defense lawyer started again.

James glanced at the lawyer, then scanned the faces of those in the audience, making sure he had everyone's attention. "I do not believe that," James started. Great gasps were heard from the courtroom. Everyone was in shock that Jesus's own brother appeared to be denying him. His serious gaze fell upon the many people in the courtroom again, waiting for quiet. A hush fell over the crowd as they waited with great eagerness to hear what he would say next.

"I know that he is the Son of God, the very Christ. I know this, not because he was my brother, but by the Holy Spirit, whose purpose it is to testify of Christ."

The courtroom remained silent except for whispered murmurs heard from the prosecution. They seemed to be preparing for their rebuttal—conjuring up what to do next. Some of them were glaring at James with angry looks.

"And what tells you that this is true?" the defense attorney urged him on.

As James looked at the lawyer, purposefully he began.

My Brother's Work

(The Testimony of James the Brother of Jesus)

There was something special in my brother,
Something more than even I could see.
He showed greater kindness than any other.
He had healing power in his hands.
He lived a life free from any sin,
Walking on this earth he helped create.
He willingly gave his precious life;
He always knew that this would be his fate.

Chorus:
I asked him not to leave me;
I wished that he could stay.
He put his arms around me,
And this is what he said:
"I must fulfill my Father's plan;
For this reason I came to earth
Which he and I created for mankind.
Now go and do as I've commanded you,
Caring for my sheep.
Follow me! Follow me and ye shall live.

Jeremy's mouth fell open in shock. Another person had masterfully displayed his conviction and testimony that Jesus is the Savior—another person who was intimately connected and associated with Jesus. *Could they both be fabricating this to protect their son and brother? Were they both fooled into believing in him?* Jeremy continued, deep in his thoughts. *Could this really be the brother of Jesus? I have read the book of James in the New Testament and heard this man's powerful testimony and knowledge of the gospel. I have heard his testimony of Jesus being the Christ in the scriptures. Why don't I believe that Jesus is the Christ? Is it simply because I have been afflicted with difficult trials?*

His thoughts were suddenly interrupted by an angry outburst from one of the prosecuting lawyers. "Are all of your witnesses going to be relatives of Jesus? All of them have a vested interest in his protection. We know that his family revered him as the Christ. But we know they do this to protect him because he is their kin. They have to protect him in order to preserve their family name. Yes, this was a persuasive testimony from someone who has lost his brother, but it is all in order to protect a loved one. We will concede that all of Jesus's family will profess that he is the Christ, but we will not accept the declaration of his family as valid. Is the defense to waste the entire day of this court bringing one family member after another to testify?"

James shook his head sadly. "I speak the truth—the truth that I learned from my brother. The truth that has been testified by the prophets of old, even your forefathers. Every prophet before Jesus's birth has spoken of him. If you can't see this, you do not understand the scriptures or your mind is clouded and beyond understanding.

JEREMY'S *Christmas* JOURNEY

You are as those of whom my brother spoke, those who 'seeing see not; and hearing hear not.' I do not defend my family name, but I do defend my brother, my Savior, who has died that I might live—"

"Silence! You will only speak when spoken to in this court," came the rebuke from the judge. The judge gave an approving nod to the prosecution, as if to indicate he was on their side.

"Take him out of the court." The judge motioned to the soldiers to obey his order, and then he looked at the defense lawyers with anger and disgust burning in his eyes. As the soldiers removed James from the courtroom, the judge spoke, "Might I ask the defense to call witnesses other than family members from this time forward? I am a busy and important man and desire to see the end of this trial."

"Yes, Your Honor," the defense responded. "We call him who once was blind but now sees, all because of the healing power of Christ, Bartimaeus."

An old man who appeared nervous and frightened was escorted into the courtroom. His skin was wrinkly and weathered, a sunbaked golden-brown color. He hung his head low, with his eyes completely focused on the ground beneath him, as though he was unwilling to look into the eyes of those in the courtroom. His dark brown hair partially hid his face because of his posture, making it difficult to see his eyes. He was dressed in ragged and dirty clothes, which were well-worn, with the occasional hole. He could easily pass as one of the beggars who sat daily at the temple.

He timidly made the short walk to the front and sat down at the witness platform. He had a mournful countenance about him, as though stricken with great sorrow. Jeremy looked at him, trying to examine the man's eyes and wondering whether the forlorn look was because he was mourning Jesus's death or because he was here to testify. Jeremy hoped to see some physical evidence that this man was formerly blind, looking for discernible scars, or perhaps cloudiness. He searched for any reminder of the man's blindness but was unsuccessful in detecting any remnants of blindness or ill health in the man's deep brown eyes.

Bartimaeus looked up for an instant, quickly surveyed the crowd, and then returned his gaze to the ground. He appeared to Jeremy like any other man he would see on the street, save for the ragged clothes. *This man is very ordinary*, Jeremy thought.

The defense began their questioning, "Sir, can you see me?"

"Why, of course I can. I haven't been blind for years now, since the day I met this Jesus for whom I am here to testify." The man's demeanor changed, no longer sad and forlorn. Now his shoulders were back, his stature was fully erect, his body appeared full of strength. It looked as if he was modifying his posture to look more respectable.

"What color is my cloak then?" the lawyer asked.

"It is brown," said Bartimaeus in a disgusted tone. He obviously was not pleased with being doubted and tested.

"I object!" roared one of the prosecuting lawyers. "How are we to know that this man was blind before? Who is here to attest to that? How do we know that this is not just more deception created by the defense to make us believe this account? I ask that the court no

JEREMY'S *Christmas* JOURNEY

longer be encumbered by this man and he be removed from the court immediately."

"I agree," started the judge. "We have no evidence that this man was ever blind, so how can he witness to the efficacy of this Jesus's power? Please remove him from the court, soldiers."

The soldiers moved hastily toward the witness stand, ready to fulfill orders to remove someone from the court for the second time this day. Just as they reached Bartimaeus and extended their hands to carry him out of the courtroom, he stood tall, and his eyes filled with intensity. He held his hand out to the soldiers in a motion to stop.

"Do not touch me, for I have come to deliver a message, and God will not allow you to harm or remove me until I have uttered the words he commands me to speak," Bartimaeus said. He remained with his hand held out firmly, waiting for the soldiers' reaction.

The soldiers stopped suddenly and looked at one another as if to see if one would dare make a move to grab the witness. Both of them were unsure of what they should do, neither daring to touch him. They looked at the judge as if he would give them reprieve of his command or offer further instructions, but none came. The judge was also in awe, uncertain of what to do next. He did not want to appear weak, yet he could not muster the strength to move his tongue to speak. His face betrayed the confusion he felt.

The soldiers backpedaled slightly, believing the judge's lack of response to be a reversal of their orders. The judge was amazed that such a weak and timid man as Bartimaeus could prevent two strong soldiers from completing a direct order. The judge nervously stroked his beard as he pondered whether the witness was telling the truth or was simply attempting to use any means of self-preservation necessary. He stared at the witness speechlessly, examining him carefully and hesitating to make a decision.

Bartimaeus realized he was going to be left unmolested, so he began to speak, "One day I was by the highway, begging as usual. I was seeking for compassion and mercy from those who passed by, simply hoping for some food or money to exchange for food. I heard a commotion. Many people were crowding the highway, seeking a glimpse of someone. My ears are very sharp, able to hear sounds from greater distances than most, because my sense of hearing strengthened to compensate for my inability to see. I heard someone say that Jesus and his disciples were coming. I had heard the rumors of his power to heal, so I pushed forward, crying out for mercy. For a moment, I feared that I might be trampled under the feet of the multitude. Then I felt hands grip my shoulders firmly, harshly pulling me away from the multitude as they pled for me to be quiet. As these men tried to force me away from the road, I began to cry out even louder. At last Jesus took notice of me and called me forward. I threw off my coat and moved in the direction of his voice. This kind man took me gently by the hand and asked me what I desired of him. I had faith that he could heal me, so I boldly stated that I desired to receive my sight. He declared that my faith had made me whole, and immediately I received my sight. I know this is an amazing tale, but it is true, and I know that only the power of God could have given me my sight."

JEREMY'S *Christmas* JOURNEY

Tears gathered in Bartimaeus's eyes as he gazed upon those who were mesmerized by what he was saying. He had been kicked out of the synagogues after receiving his sight, all because he would not deny that Jesus had healed him. He looked briefly at the judge, then again at the soldiers, and straightened his posture, erect and unyielding.

Eyes That Now See
(The Testimony of Bartimaeus)

All my life's been full of darkness
But I have gained my sight for sure.
I went through life in blackness
All my life I thought I'd endure.

I was told about a man who had the power,
Power that healed so much more.
I sought out this man so earnestly
Hoping my sight he'd restore.

And, oh, the sight I had been missing
For all these many years.
When I found the man I sought,
His gentle hands removed my fears.

Though I had no sight to see him
I felt the power in his touch
As he placed his hands upon me,
My eyes were opened to see.

"Go thy way," he said to me.
"Thy faith has made thee whole."
And for the first time in all my life,
My sight was no longer dull.

JEREMY'S *Christmas* JOURNEY

I saw the sky, I saw the trees,
I saw all he helped create.
I know he's the Christ. I know he is.
In my mind there's no debate.

And, oh, the sight I had been missing
For all these many years.
When I found the man I sought,
His gentle hands removed my fears.

Though I had no sight to see him
I felt the power in his touch
When he placed his hands upon me
My eyes were opened to see.

He healed me by his power;
By his power I can see.
I'll follow his example
For like him I want to be.

SCOTT A. JOHNSON

Bartimaeus sat back down as if a big burden had been removed from his shoulders. He sobbed, his body shaking uncontrollably, and placed his head in his hands. He wiped the tears from his eyes and cheeks with the hem of his garment, then stood again. He looked toward the soldiers, who still appeared frozen in place. They seemed to be debating internally whether they should touch him or not. Then he stared at the judge as if asking for permission to be excused. The judge only looked back in wonderment. Bartimaeus stepped down from the witness platform and walked toward the closed door. Without looking back, he opened the door, pausing only briefly to let out a deep sigh, and then stepped outside.

The courtroom remained silent in astonishment. It was evident no one knew what to do next. Jeremy stared at the open door to the courtroom, filled with admiration for what Bartimaeus had just done. An old man had faced trained soldiers to express heartfelt testimony. Jeremy's heart was beating quickly, whether from the witness's testimony or from the excitement of the situation he couldn't tell. He looked toward the prosecution, recognizing they had not had the chance to examine or question the witness, though Jeremy didn't think this would have done any good for their case. It seemed to Jeremy that even the prosecutors were afraid to articulate a rebuttal, for fear had gripped them also.

A defense lawyer looked around the courtroom and realized he had a perfect opportunity to expound upon what just happened. He turned toward the multitude and began to speak.

"We have just witnessed the powerful testimony of just one of the

JEREMY'S *Christmas* JOURNEY

many people Jesus healed. Jesus spent his whole life in our service. He went about healing all manner of disease and sickness. This was not accomplished by the earthly means of doctors or medicines, but by priesthood power. By simply touching the hem of his garment, a woman with a disease involving her blood was healed. Her faith, coupled with his power, healed her and made her whole, while physicians, despite their knowledge and medicines, were unable to exact any cure.

"While in Capernaum, a man afflicted with palsy was brought to Jesus. He healed this man also, after giving him something even more important: forgiveness of his sins." Some murmurs and hisses of blaspheme were heard among the crowd and the prosecuting lawyers.

The defense lawyer looked around the room again as if asking for quiet and then continued speaking. "He healed even those who stood not in his presence. When the Roman centurion beseeched him to heal his servant, Jesus offered to go to the centurion's house and perform the cure, but the centurion forbade him. Jesus then told the centurion that because he had such great faith, the centurion's servant would be healed as he desired. The centurion traveled home and found his servant well; in fact, his servant had been healed the very moment Jesus spoke it.

"There are innumerable accounts just like these—accounts of Jesus using his heavenly power to heal. Unfortunately, there are so many instances of healing that we have insufficient time to convey each of them. But we have brought another person here this day who benefited from Christ's healing power: Lazarus, who once was dead but now lives."

The lawyer looked at the prosecution and paused for a lengthy moment as if waiting for them to speak. "With no reply from the prosecution, if it pleases you, Your Honor, we call Lazarus to the stand as our next witness."

The judge did not say anything but simply nodded and motioned for them to bring him in. The soldiers motioned through the still-open door for Lazarus to come inside. He walked slowly and deliberately to the witness platform, keeping his eyes set upon it and focused on the task that lay before him. The courtroom was full of whisperings. Many in the courtroom knew of the rumors that Lazarus had been dead, and possibly even placed in the sepulcher, before being raised by Jesus. At first the prosecuting lawyers wanted to object under similar circumstances as with Bartimaeus, but they quickly decided against it. Lazarus sat on the witness stand waiting for his first question.

"Lazarus, how did you know Jesus?" the defense began.

"I spent many hours at the feet of the Master. He was a close friend, and a friend of my sisters Mary and Martha. I had meals with him, walked side by side with him, but most important, learned the truth of the gospel from him."

"Was he an ordinary man?" the defense continued.

"Not ordinary. No, not ordinary at all. He had more wisdom than any other person I have ever known, wisdom not only beyond his years but also beyond all earthly knowledge. He was kinder than any other person I know. He was the type of person who always knew exactly what to say to make you feel better about yourself."

JEREMY'S *Christmas* JOURNEY

"If the prosecution has no objections, we will let Lazarus tell his story," one of the defense lawyers said as he looked dubiously at the prosecutors. There was no response, so he motioned for Lazarus to proceed. "Go ahead, sir."

A Man Arisen

(The Testimony of Lazarus)

I am a man arisen
From the power of death.
I was able to come forth
At my friend's request.

I am a man awakened,
Uniting body and soul.
All to the glory of his Father
by his mercy I am whole.

He had the pow'r to raise me
But I did not understand how.
I testify he's Jesus.
This I surely know.
I'll testify he's Jesus.
This I surely know.

I have been saved by his love,
As he gave me one more chance.
And with that chance I'll witness
That he's the Son of God.

Every day I'm living,
I dedicate to him.

JEREMY'S *Christmas* JOURNEY

I'll live my life with purpose
In eternal debt to him.

And I will never revoke
This promise I have made.
He is the Christ, my Savior—
This I will always say.

I am a man arisen.

Noisy whisperings were heard among the crowd, who were obviously engrossed in conversation and debating the truthfulness of Lazarus's testimony. The story of a man being raised from the dead was almost too impossible to believe. Could he really have once been dead and now be alive again? Could Jesus really have had power over death? Even the judge stood in awe of the testimony.

The prosecution could tell that their case was hanging by a thread, so they quickly tried to refute the testimony of Lazarus.

"Are we to believe that you were dead and are now arisen?" one lawyer asked, laughing loudly. "How ignorant do you think the people before you are? You have no proof that you were dead and that this man, Jesus, called you forth from the grave. This is preposterous and impossible to believe, as is the whole story of Jesus—that a God would come upon this earth and intermingle with men, then die to save us from our sins. I say that this whole report is a lie. A lie fabricated to make men fearful and join the church this Jesus created.

"Judge, I beseech you, listen to reason and judge for us that this Jesus was no more than a fictional legend told to children at bedtime."

The lawyer had masterfully spun some doubt on the powerful testimony of Lazarus. He was cunning, and under direct orders from the high priest himself to manage this trial. He had been chosen among the many lawyers because of his expertise and craftiness. He also knew great financial reward, as well as praise, awaited him if he achieved a successful verdict.

The judge looked at Lazarus. "You are dismissed," he said forcefully, waving his hand robustly toward the courtroom door.

JEREMY'S *Christmas* JOURNEY

Lazarus walked from the witness platform with his head held high. It was clear by his face that he knew he had defended the man who had raised him from the dead and that his testimony had a profound effect on those present to hear it. The change in the disposition of those present was unmistakable. He suspected the crowd was there at the behest of the Great Sanhedrin and had all been bribed to protest against Jesus. His testimony had flustered the prosecution into asking for a hasty judgment. A slight smile emerged on his lips as he neared the place where Jeremy was.

He stopped and looked directly at Jeremy and gave him a wink. Then he whispered, "He lived and still lives." After this, he quickly turned toward the door and left the courtroom.

Jeremy sat, aghast, not sure what to believe. The burning he felt in his bosom earlier was growing stronger. It had now filled his entire body with warmth, as if warm oil were being poured over his body. He felt full of contrasting emotions, wanting to cry and shout for joy at the same time.

A defense lawyer stood up, "May I proceed, your honor? We still have more witnesses to this case who must be heard."

The judge looked at the defense lawyer, then back at the prosecuting lawyer. "All witnesses must be heard so this court can make an appropriate decision. Bring in your next witness." The judge's demeanor had perceptibly softened, and Jeremy wondered if even this hardened judge was beginning to gain an assurance that Jesus was the Son of God.

The defense lawyer nodded to the judge, then spoke, "We call the woman known only as a sinner as our next witness."

The door to the courtroom opened and a woman with long, beautiful brown hair and sparkling brown eyes walked into the courtroom. Her beauty was striking; her skin looked smooth and radiant. The closer she drew to the witness platform, the more ashamed the expression on her face appeared. Jeremy thought she was walking to the platform as if she were walking to her death. Her head was hung low, and her hair partially covered her face. She reluctantly walked the rest of the way to the platform and sat down. Jeremy looked on her in pity as he wondered why a woman with such beauty would hang her head and hide it. He stared at her with great anticipation swelling within his bosom, excited to hear the account she would share.

One of the defense lawyers walked toward her and placed his hand lightly on her shoulder for comfort and then began to speak. "Are you the woman who bathed Christ's feet in your tears, wiped them with your hair, and then anointed them with ointment as he sat at meat in the house of a Pharisee?"

She didn't raise her head but answered softly. "I am she."

"Why did you do this, woman?" he continued.

"I required spiritual healing. I knew that he had the power to forgive my many sins. I no longer wished to bear the heavy burden of the sins I carried. I was certain he was the only one who could grant me the relief I was seeking." She winced slightly as she stated this, obviously uncomfortable to be publicly confessing her sins.

JEREMY'S *Christmas* JOURNEY

"This is blasphemy," shouted one of the prosecuting lawyers. "Only God himself has the power to forgive sins. Jesus had no authority to do so!"

"How little you understand about Jesus," she started timidly. "Do you not understand the scriptures that testify that Jesus was and is God, even the great I AM?" Her courage seemed to be building with every word. "He created this earth and then condescended to it, all to offer himself as a sinless sacrifice. He is God; thus, he had the power to forgive sins. He answered a similar question to yours when he healed a man stricken with the palsy. After he forgave the man's sins, he declared, 'But that ye may know that the Son of man hath power upon earth to forgive sins . . . I say unto thee arise and take up thy couch,' and the man was healed of the palsy." She finally raised her head so that all could see her face, which was filled with tears. "I am grateful that he showed mercy to me, despite my many sins. He didn't condemn or accuse me. He didn't punish me, despite the reality that it was within his right to punish me to satisfy justice—for I had sinned. Instead he was merciful, forgiving me and charging me to go forward and sin no more. Without him, I would have no opportunity to repent—to be made clean again. I would be forever unclean and shut out of his presence. Because he died, we all may live, and by that I mean repent. Because of his resurrection, we all freely receive immortality."

The defense lawyer raised his cloak with his free hand and wiped the tears off her face tenderly. He took great care to offer her the support and comfort necessary.

45

SCOTT A. JOHNSON

"Can you continue with your testimony?" he asked.

"Yes. Yes I can." She looked up with great resolve. "I am ready to tell my story. It is the least that I can do for him, for I will never be able to truly repay him."

Whole Again

(The Testimony of the Woman Known as a Sinner)

Mine is a story of shame,
Almost more than I can take.
But when I heard of Jesus,
I knew it was for my sake.

I traveled and searched to find him,
And when I found him I cried.
I felt unworthy to see him.
Overcome, I knelt by his side.

He said my sins were forgiven
As I washed his feet with my hair.
What peace and comfort filled me
As I saw in his eyes he cared.

I washed the feet of my Lord,
Bathing them with flowing tears.
He spoke of sweet forgiveness
And silenced all my fears.

I went to him as a sinner,
But I left forgiven and cleansed.
He took my burdens upon him,
And now I am whole again.

SCOTT A. JOHNSON

His spirit speaks to my soul,
Guiding me in all I do.
I know the peace of forgiveness.
I feel so clean and renewed.

Jesus is my Redeemer,
He is my Savior, my King.
I'll never forget his mercy
As songs of praise I sing.

I went to him as a sinner,
But I left forgiven and cleansed.
He took my burdens upon him
And now I am whole again.

I cast my burdens upon him.
My spirit is whole again.

JEREMY'S *Christmas* JOURNEY

She humbly bowed her head again and raised her hands to her face, covering the tears that were steadily flowing. Her emotions now took over, and she cried uncontrollably. Her body was visibly trembling as she released copious sobs. Jesus Christ had affected her life profoundly, and the debt she felt to him made her unable to restrain her emotions when she talked about him. He had changed her life, and changed it for the better. He offered her an escape from the sins that chained her down, releasing her from a great burden. Now forgiven of her sins by the Lord, she received her freedom—freedom from the sins she yearned to forget and leave in the past.

She knew that her purpose to proclaim Jesus as the Savior had been accomplished, and she did not wish to be under scrutiny any longer. She wanted to go back to her little-known life and live as normally as she could. The defense lawyer sensed her desire to leave and took her by the hand, helping her to her feet. Her body seemed weak, as though she were physically and emotionally exhausted. He held her elbow and motioned for the other defense lawyer to help. He quickly came to her aid, and they assisted her to the door of the courtroom, each supporting her under an arm. From there she gathered what strength she could and walked out of the courtroom.

As Jeremy considered what she had said, his thoughts moved to his own life. He considered all the wrongs he had committed over the years and how he would love to have them removed from his book of life. He wished at that very moment to get upon his knees and ask for forgiveness for his sins, to ask for forgiveness for ever doubting the existence and divinity of Jesus Christ.

His heart was pounding against his rib cage like a bass drum, so hard that he felt it would burst out of his chest at any moment. A hard lump formed in his throat, which made it difficult to swallow. His eyes filled with tears, which then traveled slowly down his cheeks. He was receiving a mighty change, the mighty change that occurs in all who seek the truth about the Savior. At this instant, he too wanted to approach the witness platform to defend Jesus. He wanted to testify that Christ lives and that he is the Savior of all mankind. Somehow he knew this was true, where before he had not wanted to allow these feelings to erupt as they were now.

Just as he thought he could muster the faith and strength to overcome his disability and walk to the witness platform, he heard a booming voice from the back of the courtroom echoing through the open door.

"Am I too late . . . too late to testify?"

"No, lieutenant, you are right on time," the defense lawyer answered, smiling slightly at the man while motioning him forward with a wave of his hand.

"We call Lieutenant Tiberius of Caesar's Royal Army as our next witness," he continued.

The man was fully dressed in the traditional Roman military attire. His bulging muscles showed through the garments that he was wearing. His arms proudly displayed the battle scars he had received during years of service to the Roman Empire. He took off his helmet and placed it under his right arm as he strode gallantly toward the witness platform. He had a commanding presence and obviously had authority. The soldiers near the judge came to attention as Tiberius came forward. He briefly nodded to them, recognizing their respectful showing.

Tiberius removed his sword and leaned it against the wall behind the witness stand, set his helmet on the floor next to his feet, and then sat down. Many in the audience were astounded. A Roman soldier had come before them to testify for a Jew. This was unheard of and could possibly get this soldier in serious trouble with Caesar. This soldier was risking much and placing himself at great peril to testify in this matter. Not only could he lose his position in Caesar's army, but he could also be executed for treason against Rome.

"Please state your name for the court's records, Lieutenant," the defense lawyer started.

"I am Lieutenant Tiberius of Caesar's royal army, formerly of Pilate's royal guard, a soldier who once worked the crucifix at Calvary's Hill."

"Were you present the day that Jesus was crucified?" the defense asked.

The soldier grimaced slightly, as if in pain. "Sadly, I was. I participated in the scourging and crucifying of Jesus. I was the primary soldier in charge of carrying out Pilate's orders that day."

"Then why are you here to testify on his behalf?" the defense replied.

"I feel obligated to. I have experienced a mighty change since that day. I feel I must do something to reconcile the greatest wrong I have ever committed, that of crucifying my Lord."

The courtroom groaned with shock, amazed that someone who had participated in the crucifixion of Jesus would now stand to testify on his behalf. Those in the courtroom exchanged stunned glances before the room erupted into disorder. The judge stood and commanded that the crowd remain silent.

The defense lawyer waited until the crowd was quiet again and then continued his questioning. "Will you please recount what occurred that day?"

The soldier frowned and groaned as he began to describe the events. "I received orders from Pilate that I was to scourge and crucify a man. This was nothing unusual. I supposed I was punishing another criminal who had been condemned to death.

"I took Jesus to the scourging room to carry out my orders. On the way I passed through the common hall, where most of my soldiers were assembled. I ordered my men to strip him of his raiment in preparation for scourging. As is common, my men made a sport of this, taunting him and slapping him with the backs of their hands. I am reluctant to admit that at the time it gave me pleasure to humiliate and embarrass him.

"I had heard that he was supposed to be a king, or at least claimed to be the king of the Jews, so I ordered my men to place a scarlet robe on his shoulders and a crown of thorns on his head. To complete his mock kingly attire, I placed a reed in his right hand. After this, we disrespectfully bowed the knee before him, pretending to worship him. One of my men even hit him over the head with the reed. As directed, I commanded that he be whipped, but not the normal

JEREMY'S *Christmas* JOURNEY

whipping men receive. I allowed the whipping to continue beyond what any other man had ever experienced. I was truthfully amazed that he was able to survive the beating I ordered to be inflicted upon him.

"When I felt we had properly humiliated him, I placed his torn and tattered clothing back on him and forced him to carry the upper beam of his cross to Golgotha. Along the path, we compelled a Cyrenian man named Simon to carry the beam to the cross. When we arrived at the hill, we nailed Jesus to the cross, one nail in each palm, and one nail in each wrist to avoid tearing through the flesh of his palms. He was placed between two other men we were crucifying that day. As he hung there, my soldiers cast lots for what was left of his clothing. Pilate even had us nail an inscription above his head that read, 'THIS IS JESUS, THE KING OF THE JEWS.'

"About the sixth hour of the day, great darkness began to encompass the land, and a great storm emerged. The storm continued to build force, and it became clear that this was a potentially injurious storm.

"About the ninth hour, I was concerned that we would be caught in a raging storm, so I gave the order to break the legs of those being crucified. I was hoping this would speed up their deaths. We broke the legs of the two men being crucified with Jesus first, but when we came to Jesus to break his legs, he was already dead.

"To make sure, one of my soldiers pierced Jesus's side with his spear, causing great amounts of blood and water to gush forth. Immediately following, the earth began to quake more than I had ever experienced. It felt as though the whole earth were violently shaking, and it caused me to fall to the earth. I felt as though the earth would swallow me whole. I feared for my life and thought I was doomed to destruction. At this point I realized that Jesus must have been a righteous man, that the earth was trying to punish us for killing her Creator.

"When the shaking stopped, I gathered my men and retreated to the common hall. I was agonizing over what had just occurred, what I had been a part of, when Joseph of Arimathaea approached and requested to take the body of Jesus. I knew Joseph must have known Jesus, so I asked him if he could teach me the things that Jesus taught. My heart was considerably troubled, and I had a great desire to know more about him.

"Joseph was wary about believing my change of heart, supposing I had ulterior motives, but he finally consented. After receiving instruction for many days, I made the difficult decision to be baptized, something I have kept hidden until this very day."

"What caused your change of heart?" the defense queried.

Tiberius looked around the courtroom, then specifically at the prosecution. He did so, questioning whether they were relishing the idea of putting him on trial next. He received contemptuous glares back. His face was solemn as he turned back to the crowd. His grimace revealed the varied emotions he was struggling with. He exhaled deeply as if to demonstrate he had made up his mind to speak.

A Changed Man

(The Testimony of the Roman Soldier)

I'm not proud of the story that's mine,

For what I did, I'll dearly pay.

I knew not whom I whipped and scourged.

Now my soul is racked with pain.

While on the cross, he spoke words never heard.

He pled for our souls, and thunder roared.

I fell down, frightened and afraid.

True forgiveness now I seek from him.

He died that day on Calvary's hill;

This Jesus whom I saw.

I spit and mocked and tortured him

Like those who broke the law.

It was I who nailed him to the cross.

And forced a crown of thorns upon his head.

I laughed and scorned him as he suffered there

Till the moment I knew he was dead.

Ah. Ah.

I begged the Father for his mercy

For crucifying his perfect Son.

I finally understood who Jesus was

And lamented all that I had done.

SCOTT A. JOHNSON

I had no doubt I was doomed to hell
For the things I'd done to my Lord.
At his feet I wept most bitterly
As I begged for mercy from my God.
Ah. Ah.

JEREMY'S *Christmas* JOURNEY

As a Roman soldier, Tiberius had been trained to keep his emotions in check even in the most arduous circumstances, but as he finished his testimony, the corners of his eyes were moist with tears. It was an incredible sight to see a muscular and powerful soldier, one who had surely seen and taken part in unspeakable atrocities, showing such emotion. Surprisingly, it did not make him appear weak. The tears seemed appropriate—they permitted him a release of bottled up emotions he so urgently needed.

Tiberius knew that the acts he had committed that day on Calvary's Hill were almost unforgivable. He knew that better now than ever before. But he took comfort in Jesus's selfless act and the words he had spoken on the cross in Tiberius's behalf. Christ's sacrifice gave him hope that even he could be forgiven of all his sins, despite the awfulness of the act he had committed. The teachings he had received from Joseph taught him that the Atonement applied to all men who are willing to accept it.

He sat on the witness platform hunched over, with one hand rubbing his forehead worriedly. It was plain to see in his expression the agony he was feeling for the acts that he had committed years ago. The pain seemed fresh and close to the surface. Discussing his part in Christ's crucifixion caused him to look defeated and sorrowful. Though he believed he had been forgiven for his acts, he still suffered with regret and a pang of guilt.

The prosecuting lawyers had their hands to their faces in abhorrence. Their lips were tight, and their eyes were narrowed in anger. It was easy to perceive from their body language and behavior that the strength of their case was quickly vanishing. Every witness in the courtroom today had produced a profound effect on all who were present, but this man who participated in the crucifixion of Jesus and now was testifying on Jesus's behalf was devastating to their case. A Roman soldier's word was unimpeachable. The lawyers' minds were working frantically to find a way to counteract this overwhelming effect, but they were unsuccessful.

Jeremy sat quietly in the audience, filled to the brim with emotion. His heart was beating at a quickened pace, and he felt short of breath. He felt an overwhelming spirit consuming him, prompting him to stand and testify on Jesus's behalf, to testify for the man who only moments earlier he had doubted.

The judge cleared his throat. "Does the prosecution wish to question the lieutenant?"

There was no response from any of them. They looked at the judge forlornly until one shook his head slightly. The judge looked at Tiberius and nodded respectfully. Tiberius understood this as permission to leave and stood to gather his belongings.

A defense lawyer moved forward and draped his arm around the soldier, whispering something inaudible to the others present. The defense lawyer had tears streaming down his face, as did many others in the multitude. Tiberius straightened his back, slowly gaining some of his composure, as they walked toward the back of the courtroom. His helmet was tucked tightly under his left arm. He kept his eyes looking straight ahead at the door he would leave through.

Just then Jeremy felt an immense force pulling him. He felt like he

JEREMY'S *Christmas* JOURNEY

was being pulled from the courtroom. An intense light, greater than the noonday sun, gradually overtook the room until it was so full of this light he could no longer see. After a short time, the light began to diminish and gathered directly in front of him. Jeremy observed his surroundings. He was no longer in the courtroom. He had been transported to another unfamiliar place. His eyes were still adjusting from the bright light, making it difficult to tell exactly where he was. As his eyes adjusted further, he could barely make out the outline of a man directly in front of him. The light was radiating from the man as if he were the source of it.

Jeremy squinted hard and was able to make out the features of the man's face. The man's eyes were inviting and comforting, and his face was filled with compassion and love. He was wearing a brilliantly white robe that covered all but his feet, hands, and face. The man smiled as he moved toward Jeremy. Normally Jeremy would have felt fear, but he was overcome with peace. The man reached out his hand and gently touched Jeremy's legs. With the man so close, Jeremy was finally able to discern who it was in front of him. The Savior of the world stood before him. The man he had doubted. The man whose trial he had been witnessing.

Tears streamed down Jeremy's cheeks. He opened his mouth to speak, to ask for forgiveness for ever doubting him, but his throat had such a large lump, he was unable to speak. Jeremy instead summoned a weak smile to communicate as he gazed into Christ's engaging eyes. Jeremy tried to speak again, but no words came out. He closed his mouth and swallowed hard. Jesus looked into Jeremy's eyes tenderly and smiled as if he knew what Jeremy desired to say. Jeremy noticed the light around Jesus was gradually softening. Jesus was ascending toward the sky. Soon he could no longer see Jesus, only a remnant of the brilliant light remained visible.

A powerful force was pulling Jeremy again. He felt as if he were being sucked through the hose of a vacuum. His surroundings were a blur momentarily. When the feeling ended, Jeremy realized he was in the courtroom again.

A defense lawyer was standing near the judge, speaking. "Your Honor, we feel as though our case has been well established. We believe we have proved unequivocally that, in fact, Jesus was the Christ, our Savior, our Redeemer, and the literal Son of God. You can see how many have attested to his divine character and existence. Each witness has masterfully shared a credible and compelling testimony with us today, and we believe no more witnesses are necessary to prove our case. One needs only search the prophets to find the only conclusion that can be made, that Jesus was the Son of God, the One prepared from the beginning to be our Savior. All may know this, as I do, and as the witnesses do. It requires faith and prayer, but all may know. We now rest our case . . ."

"Wait!" echoed a cry from the middle of the courtroom. "Please wait!"

All eyes turned to the area the voice originated from. There was Jeremy, his hands clenched tightly to his side, standing rigid and full of vigor. He was so full of emotion he did not even realize that he was standing by his own power, a feat he had not accomplished in many

JEREMY'S *Christmas* JOURNEY

years. The congregation examined him carefully as if this was the first time they were aware of his presence.

"I would like to add my testimony to those who have spoken before me," Jeremy said as his lip quivered and his eyes blinked frantically to displace the tears that were blurring his vision.

The defense lawyer looked at the boy in shock, unsure of what to do. He looked toward the judge, who had a similarly perplexed look on his face. Finally, the judge nodded, and the defense motioned for Jeremy to come forward.

To Be More Like Him

(The Testimony of Jeremy)

I doubted his truthfulness,
Wondered if he was real.
All my prayers went unanswered.
Thought I'd never be healed.

I felt so abandoned—
All alone by myself—
That Christ had no power
To give me my health.

Warmth I felt on my shoulder.
My desire was renewed.
I lifted my head to look,
Anger gone, but still so confused.

A man stood clothed in white,
His hand outstretched to me.
His presence gave me comfort,
He lifted me from my knees.

I knew him instantly,
My Savior spoke so clear.
"I am here to help you!"
His words dissolved my fears.

JEREMY'S *Christmas* JOURNEY

"I have finished my task,
Though very hard to bear.
On the cross I bled and died,
To show how much I care.

"The nails the soldiers drove,
The spear that pierced my side,
I bore for all mankind
So all might live that die.

"Know that I'm always here,
I'll make your burdens light.
Just kneel down and ask me,
My strength will be your might.

"As you face adversity,
Remember this, my word.
Two can conquer anything,
If one is me, your Lord."

His words gave me comfort;
They were meant to be my guide.
I will try to be more like him
So with him I may abide.

Abruptly Jeremy woke from sleep and realized he was falling. He hit the floor with a thud and rolled over on his back to gather his senses. Jeremy recognized he was back in his room, lying on the cold, hardwood floor. He lay there for a moment, pondering what he had experienced. Was it all real? he thought.

He became aware that he suffered no pain from landing on the uninviting floor, seemingly protected by the extraordinary warmth he was feeling. He understood this was more than physical warmth— he felt the warmth of the Savior. He knew for certain that Jesus existed and that he was his personal Savior, as well as the Savior of all mankind. Jeremy knew this without any doubt now. He had gained a personal conviction and testimony of Jesus Christ after his moving journey. He felt so much peace and comfort, more than he had ever felt before. Great gratitude swelled within his heart for the opportunity he had been granted to witness such a powerful event.

He strained to look at the clock on his nightstand, barely able to see it from his position on the floor. It was now four in the morning. It was hard for him to believe his experience had consumed so much of the night. He had been so enthralled in the proceedings it seemed only minutes had passed.

He gathered himself enough to grasp the bottom of his wheelchair. Using it for support, he labored to get back on the bed. Only, strangely, he did not struggle. He stood upon his feet, and all at once he noticed how straight and tall he was standing. He was standing on his own two feet and under his own power; something was decidedly different. He realized that he had received a miracle this night, not only a miracle of physical healing, but also a miracle of healing that only the power of Jesus can provide. He had gained a personal testimony that Jesus is the Christ, as well as a better understanding of Christ's purpose.

An enthusiastic smile appeared on Jeremy's face as he became conscious that not only would he stand taller physically, he would stand tall the rest of his life as a witness of Christ.

He peered out his bedroom window, noticing how radiant the stars appeared. They seemed to be twinkling in acknowledgment, as if they knew he had transformed. He heard a faint sound that seemed to be emanating from the heavens. He strained to hear what it was. It was singing. It sounded as though angels in heaven were rejoicing—rejoicing over a lost soul returning to the flock of the Savior. Jeremy knew the singing was for him. He smiled, listening intently as he relished the mighty change he had experienced.

Now Rejoice

(An Angel Choir)

Let the hosts of heaven now rejoice,
Assembling to sing as if one voice.
Praising the Lord, our heav'nly King.
Join with your voice and with us sing.
Now rejoice! Now rejoice!

Angelic hosts are called to sing.
Sing praises to our mighty God and King.
The one who died that all might live.
Our Advocate, his life did give.
Now rejoice! Now rejoice!

Hallelujah, to our Savior and King.
Hallelujah! Creator, Heir of all things.
Hallelujah! Now rejoice!

Praise him, our Lord, God, and King!
Shout praises! Shout praises!
Praise his name!
And proclaim that he is King!
Hallelujah!
Now rejoice!

Let the hosts of heaven now rejoice!
Assembling to sing as if one voice.

JEREMY'S *Christmas* JOURNEY

Praising the Lord our heav'nly King.

Join with your voice and with us sing.

Now rejoice! Now rejoice!

Now rejoice! For Jesus is Lord

For Jesus Christ is King!

More Than My Son
The Testimony of Mary

Scott Johnson
Lyle K. Hadlock

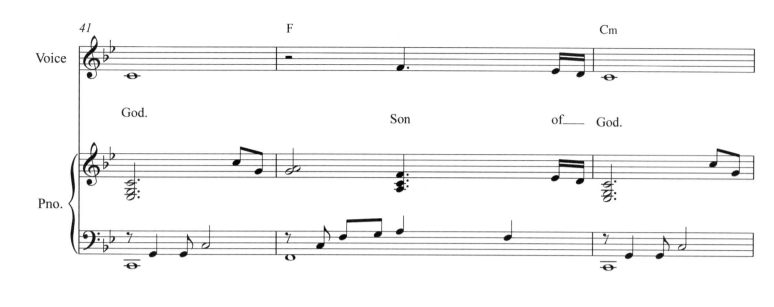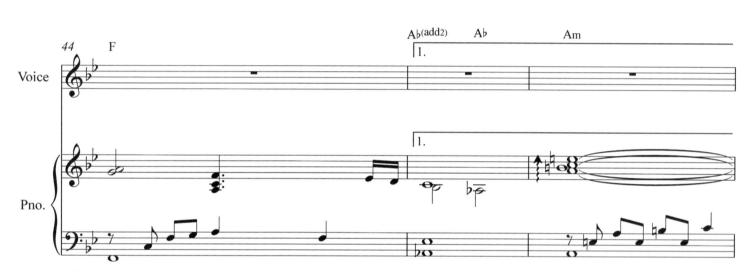

My Brother's Work
The Testimony of James

Scott Johnson
Lyle K. Hadlock

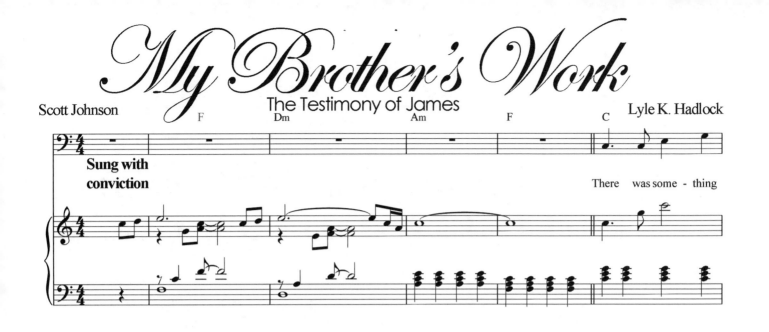
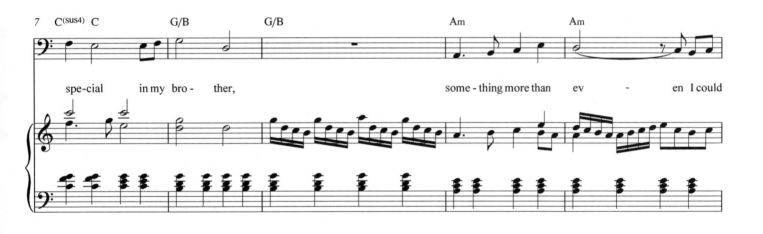

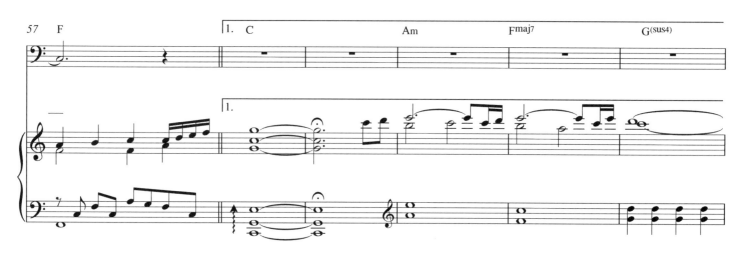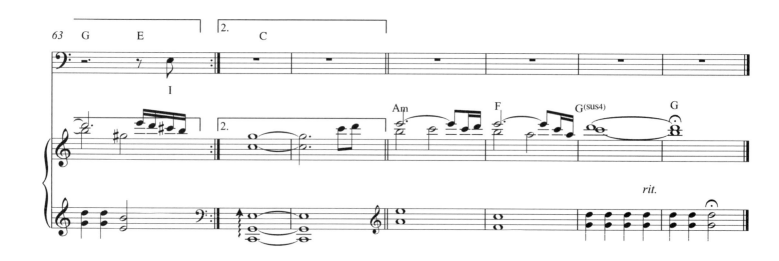

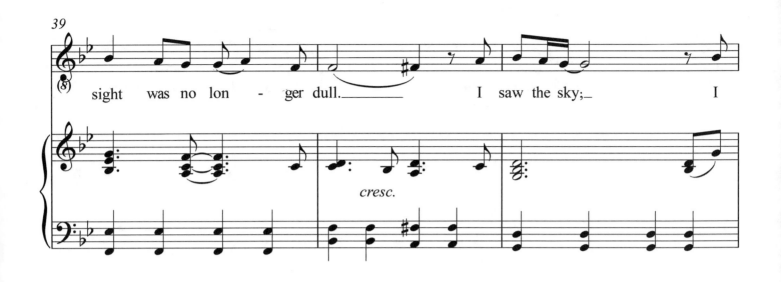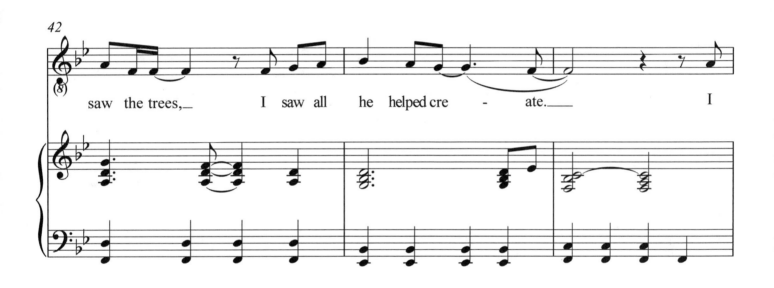

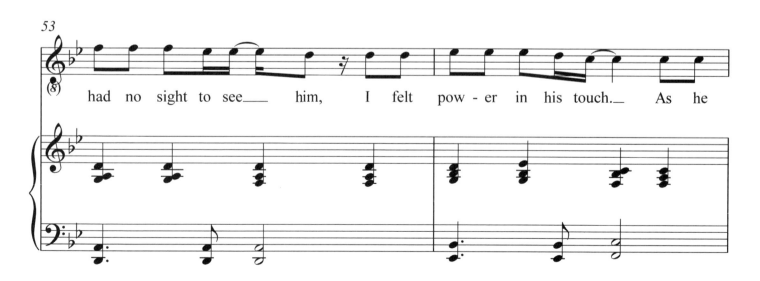

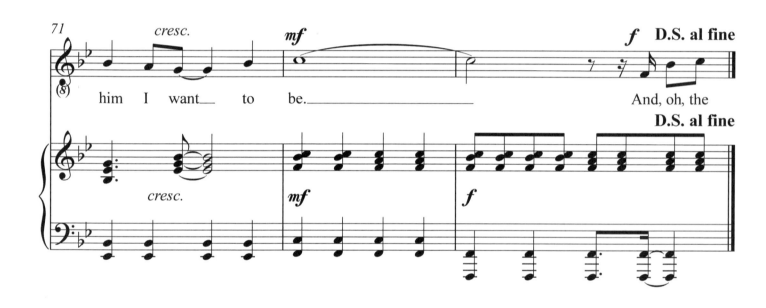

Whole Again

Scott Johnson
Julie Hawkins

The Testimony of the Woman Known Only as a Sinner

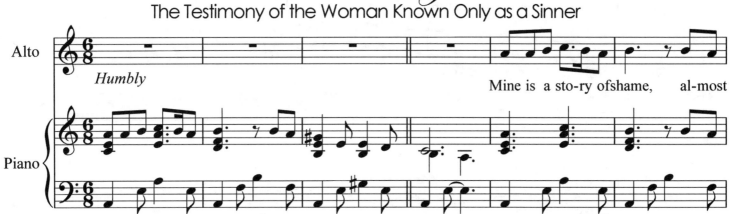
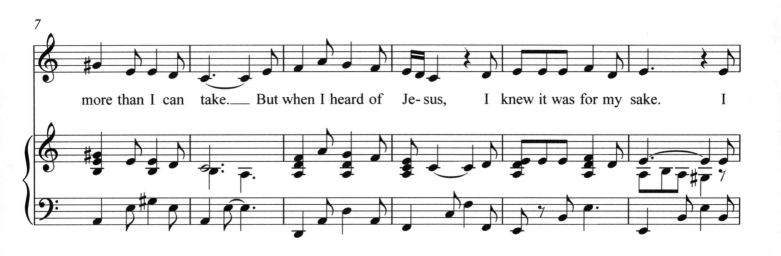

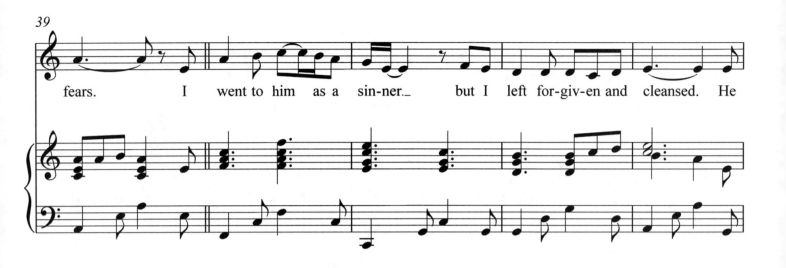

To Be More Like Him

The Testimony of Jeremy

Scott Johnson

Julie Hawkins

Jeremy singing
1st time only

mp
I. doubt-ed his truth-ful-ness. won-dered if he was real.

The Savior singing
2nd time only

mf
"I have fin-ished my task, though ve-ry hard to bear.___

All my pray'rs went un-an-swered. Thought I'd nev-er be healed.

On the cross I bled___ and died to show how much I care.___

98

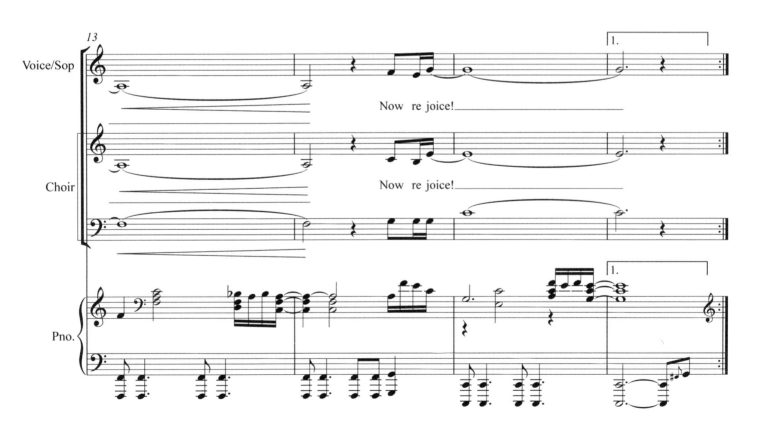

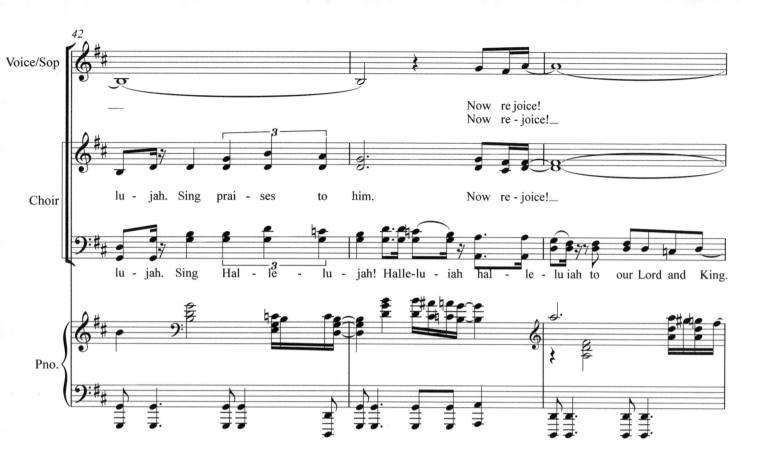

About the Author

Scott Johnson spent most of his childhood in Orem, Utah, where he gained a love for creative writing. Recognizing his potential at a young age, his teachers and family encouraged him to explore his developing writing talents.

Scott continued to craft imaginative and original stories through his teenage years and served as a yearbook writer and photographer in high school. He published his first book, *Nutrition: A Word of Wisdom*, in 2009 and has published more than 175 editorial pieces in various online publications.

Scott, his wife, and their four children reside in Utah County, where they enjoy the mountains and outdoors. Scott is regularly asked by his children to share an original story, and he gladly obliges.

About the Composers

LYLE HADLOCK SHOWED MUSICAL PROMISE AT THE AGE OF three, when he started picking out songs on the piano after hearing them played. He has recorded, arranged light orchestration, and been the pianist for seven inspirational instrumental CDs. He enjoys composing and has written two Easter Cantatas as well as various religious materials for piano and voice. Lyle is married to Jan Hadlock and is the father of three children, Kayla, Kelsie, and Jonah. His son Jonah wrote one of the songs on the Jeremy Christmas project and cowrote the choir finale ending with his father. Lyle has two beautiful granddaughters. He enlisted in the Marines at age twenty-one and went on to play clarinet and saxophone in the band. Today Lyle continues to write and arrange music and helps others put their original compositions to piano sheet music and arrangements. When he is not dabbling in music, he is known as "Brown Santa" because he delivers parcels for UPS.

*J*ULIE HAWKINS BEGAN PLAYING THE PIANO AT AGE FIVE AND added the guitar and songwriting at age twelve. She grew up in a small town on the Arizona–New Mexico border but loves living in Utah, where she can quickly get to the ski slopes on a powder day. Her guitar heroes are Dan Fogelberg, John Denver, and Guy Golightly. Julie has two amazing kids and a goofy beagle. She enjoys performing and working with other songwriters and musicians. Her debut CD, "Look at Her Now," was released in 2001.

Jonah Hadlock started playing the piano at age eight. Presently, at age seventeen, he has become an accomplished piano player. He accompanies his Maple Mountain High School choirs and fellow students for their recitals and state high school singing competitions. Jonah is also a bass in his school choir. He's made it a hobby to learn other instruments as well, such as the ukulele, bass guitar, cello, and contra bass, and he is working on the guitar. He loves to compose classical music and ballads. Jonah enjoys running and is a member of his school's varsity cross country and track teams. Jonah is the son of Lyle and Jan Hadlock. He has two sisters, Kayla and Kelsie, and two nieces, Kayla's daughters, Shelby and Mercedes.